A State of Justice

A State of Justice

by
TOM PAULIN

FABER AND FABER LIMITED
3 Queen Square London

First published in 1977
by Faber and Faber Limited
3 Queen Square London WC1
Printed in Great Britain by
The Bowering Press Ltd, Plymouth

ISBN 0 571 10982 9

FOR GITI

821·9

Contents

Acknowledgements

Some of these poems have appeared in: *Anglo-Welsh Review, Caret, Encounter, Fortnight, Gong, Honest Ulsterman, London Magazine, New Poems 1976* (P.E.N. Anthology), 'New Poems from Ulster' (BBC Radio 3), *New Statesman, Omens, Poetry Introduction 3* (Faber), *Poetry Nation, The New Review, Times Literary Supplement;* and some have also appeared in a pamphlet, *Theoretical Locations* (Ulsterman Publications).

States

That stretch of water, it's always
There for you to cross over
To the other shore, observing
The lights of cities on blackness.

Your army jacket at the rail
Leaks its kapok into a wind
That slices gulls over a dark zero
Waste a cormorant skims through.

Any state, built on such a nature,
Is a metal convenience, its paint
Cheapened by the price of lives
Spent in a public service.

The men who peer out for dawning
Gantries below a basalt beak,
Think their vigils will make something
Clearer, as the cities close

With each other, their security
Threatened but bodied in steel
Polities that clock us safely
Over this dark; freighting us.

Settlers

They cross from Glasgow to a black city
   Of gantries, mills and steeples. They begin to belong.
He manages the Iceworks, is an elder of the Kirk;
   She becomes, briefly, a cook in Carson's Army.
Some mornings, walking through the company gate,
   He touches the bonnet of a brown lorry.
It is warm. The men watch and say nothing.
   'Queer, how it runs off in the night,'
He says to McCullough, then climbs to his office.
   He stores a warm knowledge on his palm.

   Nightlandings on the Antrim coast, the movement of guns
Now snug in their oiled paper below the floors
   Of sundry kirks and tabernacles in that county.

Under the Eyes

Its retributions work like clockwork
Along murdering miles of terrace-houses
Where someone is saying, 'I am angry,
I am frightened, I am justified.
Every favour, I must repay with interest,
Any slight against myself, the least slip,
Must be balanced out by an exact revenge.'

The city is built on mud and wrath.
Its weather is predicted; its streetlamps
Light up in the glowering, crowded evenings.
Time-switches, ripped from them, are clamped
To sticks of sweet, sweating explosive.
All the machinery of a state
Is a set of scales that squeezes out blood.

Memory is just, too. A complete system
Nothing can surprise. The dead are recalled
From schoolroom afternoons, the hill quarries
Echoing blasts over the secured city;
Or, in a private house, a Judge
Shot in his hallway before his daughter
By a boy who shut his eyes as his hand tightened.

A rain of turds; a pair of eyes; the sky and tears.

Practical Values

Together, or singly, they mean nothing.
How little they have to do with love or care.
The shoaling mackerel, their silver and cobalt;
Perfected girls equipped with cunts and tits;
Soldiers, their guts triggered on wet streets.

Their massed, exact designs are so complete;
Anonymous and identical, they're shaped
By murderous authorities, built like barracks.
Servile and vicious in their uniforms,
In their skins of sleeked metal, these bodies trade.

Thinking of Iceland

Forgetting the second cod war
to go North to that island
that's four days' sailing from Hull
would be what? An escape?
Or an attempt at finding
what's behind everything?
(Too big the last question for a holiday trip.)

Still, reading the letters
they fired back to England
(one, unfortunately, to Crossman)
brings back a winter monochrome
of coast and small townships
that are much nearer home :
Doochery, the Rosses, Bloody Foreland.

An empty road over hills
dips under some wind-bent,
scrub trees, there's a bar
painted pink, some houses,
a petrol pump by a shop;
it's permanently out-of-season
here where some people live for some reason.

A cluster too small for a village,
fields waste with grey rocks
that lichens coat—hard skin
spread like frozen cultures,
green, corroded tufts that make dyes
for tweed—shuttles clack
in draughty cottages based in this sour outback.

On the signposts every place
has two names; people live
in a cold climate, a landscape
whose silence denies efforts
no one feels much like making:
when someone is building
it looks like a joke, as though they're having us on.

They poke laughing faces
through fresh wooden struts and throw
a greeting from new rafters;
on the box in the bar
a sponsored programme begins;
the crime rate is low—small sins
like poaching or drink. It's far to the border.

Now that a small factory
which cans and dries vegetables
has opened, some girls stay
and scour the county for dances.
In these bleak parishes that seem
dissolved in a grey dream
some men are busy mixing concrete, digging septics.

In winter there is work
with the council on the roads,
or with local contractors.
Each year Packy Harkin
builds a new boat, choosing
for a keel a long curving
branch from a sheltered wood where oaks grow straight.

In the dark panelled bar
through the shop, there's a faded
print of an eviction:
one constable crouches
on the thatch, the family stands
at the door, pale, while bands
of constabulary guard the whiskered bailiff.

In the top corner, clumsily,
the face of a young woman
glimmers : *The Irish patriot,*
Miss Maud Gonne. Sour smell of porter,
clutter of hens in the yard :
no docking in sagaland—
the wish got as far as this coast, then worked inland.

And yet, at Holar, striking matches
in church, trying to snap
a carved altar piece : strange figures
absent-mindedly slaughtering
prisoners; or 'exchanging politenesses'
with Goering's brother at breakfast,
was this coming-full-circle not the question they asked?

From

You've made a table you say, and are happy.
It's easy to understand where you are.
I can see you in a room we both know,
Cutting fresh wood, looking up now and then
To a window autumn light comes through.
There is a green glass float on the sill
And two stone jars we found washed by storms
On the strand. In the blueness outside, frost
And a light that, touching, makes what you see.
In that still light and silence the long hills
That ring the bay are brittle, fixed in glaze.
The island below you is a lost place
That no one can cross to in the neap,
The winter season. The tides slack,
But they never pull back; the graveyard
And ruined chapel are not to be reached now.
A priest lived there in the house when processions
Used to cross the sands slowly, in black.
Rotting boards nailed to its windows, that hermitage
Is obsolete. The light stays at that end
Of the island, catches that small, broken settlement
Where thin stones, laid flat on a humped ground,
Are carved with turnip skulls and crude bones.
A soft grass covers them and light falls.

Inishkeel Parish Church

Standing at the gate before the service started,
In their Sunday suits, the Barrets talked together,
Smiled shyly at the visitors who packed the church
In summer. A passing congregation
Who mostly knew each other, were sometimes fashionable,
Their sons at prep school, the daughters boarding.
Inside it was as neat and tight as a boat.
Stone flags and whitewashed walls, a little brass.
Old Mrs. Flewitt played the organ and Mr. Alwell
Read the lessons in an accent as sharp as salt.

O Absalom, Absalom, my son,
An hour is too long, there are too many people,
Too many heads and eyes and thoughts that clutter.

Only one moment counted with the lessons
And that was when, the pressure just too much,
You walked slowly out of that packed church
Into bright cold air.
Then, before the recognitions and the talk,
There was an enormous sight of the sea,
A silent water beyond society.

Cadaver Politic

The grey hills of that country fall away
   Like folds of skin. There are some mountains somewhere
And public parks with metal fountains.
   Rains fall and then fogs freeze, drifting
Over empty stretches of water, forts
   With broken walls on small islands.
Rafted cities smoke in the rain and sharp posts
   Have been knocked deep into flabby ground,
Thin tatters of chicken wire strung to them.
   Coffins are moored in its bays and harbours.
A damp rag, it flies several flags—
   Bunting and boneyard streamers, the badges
Of territory. In the waste, silent valleys
   Clans are at their manœuvres.
At the bottom of a cliff, on a tussock
   Of ground by a lean-to shed, a group
Of men and women huddle, watching a man
   Who tries, with damp matches, to light a board
Washed on that coast by the grey sea.

Systems

Pulsars transmit behind the stars
To future antennae.
We will hear those black spaces throbbing.
The frozen gas will get through to us.

In wooden huts on the permafrost,
Beneath those unacknowledged nowheres,
Transported bodies are broken up.

Deceased Effects

We go to auctions now and bid for things
That people once belonged to. They've shed their lives
And kept a dust that never quite scrubs off.
Unfaithful survivors, they fall to scruffy dealers,
The poor, or the ambitious young. Quaint now,
The functional metal beds the dead once woke in
When sirens went at five and mills clanked all night.

Those little bits of china that were fixed
To mantelshelves in neat front rooms, the chairs
They sat in, all the odds and ends they lived among,
Parts of a pattern that only seemed to fit,
Tell us nothing and never go for much—
Though last week there was one lot that told
Its own sparse story : a pile of photographs,
The wedding sometime, plain, unfashionable,
Six fresh-faced children behind dusty glass,
The couple older on an anniversary, and then,
Almost too pat, a mountain of wreaths on a grave,
Knocked down to someone for the frames.

A New Society

It's easy enough to regret them when they're gone.
Beds creaked on boards in the brick meadows
Somewhere above a tired earth no one had seen
Since Arkwright became a street name.

Their boxed rooms were papered with generations,
There were gas lamps, corner shops that smelt of wrapped bread,
Worn thresholds warmed by the sun and kids playing ball
Near the odd, black, Ford Popular.

Then they were empty like plague streets, their doors barred
And windows zinced. Dead lids weighted with coins,
Dead ends all of them when their families left.
Then broken terraces carried away in skips.

A man squints down a theodolite, others stretch white tapes
Over the humped soil or dig trenches that are like useful graves.
Diesel combusts as yellow bulldozers push earth
With their shields. Piledrivers thud on opened ground.

Just watching this—the laid-out streets, the mixers
Churning cement, the new bricks rising on their foundations—
Makes me want to believe in some undoctrinaire
Statement of what should be. A factual idealism.

A mummified Bentham should flourish in this soil
And unfold an order that's unaggressively civilian,
Where taps gush water into stainless sinks
And there's a smell of fresh paint in sunlit kitchens.

Where rats are destroyed and crawlies discouraged,
Where the Law is glimpsed on occasional traffic duties
And the streets are friendly with surprise recognitions.
Where, besides these, there's a visible water

That lets the sun dazzle on Bank Holidays, and where kids
Can paddle safely. There should be some grass, too,
And the chance of an unremarkable privacy,
A vegetable silence there for the taking.

A September Rising

I nearly saw them this morning.
There was rust in the beech leaves,
The branches were twisted and nude, grey
In the glistening from a blue that stretched
The subtlest, the finest of frosts.

They were there in that air,
Faintly cheeping, chittering a white
Web in the blue. Changing and staying still.
Squaddies and navvies perhaps, but
Mainly the spirit grocers.

Beyond politeness, justified;
Beyond salt bacon and rickety bells
Jangled on light doors by their betters.
The invisible purveyors of provisions,
Glad now in their fine element.

They could chicker above the trees
In the blue air, they could be
Queerly happy and seethe like sprats,
Like fresh silver in the deepest drawer.
Everywhere their names are fading,

They are taken down, stranded
Among speed, on forgotten shelves
In the back offices of new democracies;
But they live, they live again
Above brick cities which are soldiers' villages.

The Hyperboreans

Those city states staked out
On flat, thousand-acre sites
Of damp moorland
Are the theoretical locations
Most of us inhabit.

The iron-bound, leather volumes
Of political philosophies
Silting the dust
In brown country-house libraries
Are fulfilled here

(Just turning a tap on proves it).
Rough, pictish hordes scrabbling
Like bodied clouds
Drain away into our sealed ducts
From bare hills.

Though proofed against most of their
Uncivil, natural subversions,
We, too, invent,
Within bedded walls, our own
Distanced localities,

The unmapped settlements only we
Can find a way to, where a train
Stops by a sign
At the rail-head, near the new
Workers' co-op.

Helevyn the letters say. Cyrillic
Or Gaelic? The paint glistens.
Stacked with soft peat,
A line of yellow trucks shunts out
To the power-station;

While, on afforested slopes,
Chain-saws bite into spruce and fir.
The pine huts
Everyone lives in fresh keenly
Of green juniper;

Their strenuous inhabitants smile
In a chill light, then go on working.
They know all the
Objections to this bracken frontier,
Lawless, chastening;

And if their loves are seldom easy
Their only authorities are those
Black, cairnless summits,
And these their energetic combines
Are subduing.

A Just State

The children of scaffolds obey the Law.
Its memory is perfect, a buggered sun
That heats the dry sands around noon cities
    Where only the men hold hands.

The state's centre terrifies, its frontiers
Are sealed against its enemies. Shouts echo
Through the streets of this angry polity
    Whose waters might be kind.

Its justice is bare wood and limewashed bricks,
Institutional fixtures, uniforms,
The shadows of watchtowers on public squares,
    A hemp noose over a greased trap.

Gael and Protestant

'If one had to make one simple distinction, it might be that whereas English and American fiction seems to be written *puncto temporis*, out of the complexities of a moment of time, Irish fiction has a sense of the clouds flowing over the rim of the horizon, the days' procession towards World's End.' ROGER GARFITT.

Castle above the city, with its
Telephones and dungeons,
A new régime hasn't changed
The lives there much. Not that much.

Guards and constables meet
At a customs post in soft rain,
And we can expect no more
Than this official god.

The funerals and uniforms,
Occasional collusions—smile !
The hard men, who hate each other,
Are wanking in a back room.

They love, and respect, their enemies.
Obedient, like us, they've sold
Their hearts to strength. The utter
Horizons, moistened by clouds,

The deprived fields beyond
The city's clocks—our fictions
Look there, too. Crowds and
Bus tickets? It isn't enough.

On the mountains, mists hanging
To them like heroes, we think
There must be answers. Someone
Absolutely *has* to know them.

Provincial Narratives

The girl's too singular, too passionate,
For him to understand. How can she ever cross that field—
Its warm hays, a sour coolness they bring in cans—
And face him, be with him, when the man's trapped
In a facile childhood, his province of self-love?

So, in the big house, the lady of the arum lilies says,
'Come, I'll be mother. Your father is a sternness
Your mother left. Sit here with me. Kiss me,'
She orders gently. 'I will be good to you.
I will pay you to get away and then come back to me.'

He kneels at her feet. The white hands stroke his hair.
'I blame that bitch my mother. I blame
The paternal mountains and the black earth.
Some abominable collusion got me,
A bedroom huddle that was brief and vicious.'

'Don't say that. You musn't say so,' she lies.
The lilies gape. Such fear ! And softness.
A mile outside her lodge-gates, old gruffness
Goes to bed alone. His love has curdled.
His son's is for the girl's ambitious coldness,

And for her white aunt. She is the moon he follows—
The tyranny of her cheekbones, her oval eyes
That are unkind and distant, fixed on the hazing lough.
Make me older, he prays. Let me see myself
In my own mirror. Make me more perfect than she is.

In a Northern Landscape

Ingela is thin and she never smiles,
The man is tall and wears the same subdued colours.
Their accents might be anywhere, both seem perfect
And spend only the winter months here.
They own a stone cottage at the end of a field
That slopes to rocks and a gunmetal sea.

Their silence is part of the silence at this season,
Is so wide that these solitaries seem hemmed in
By a distance of empty sea, a bleak mewing
Of gulls perched on their chimney, expecting storm.
They sit in basket chairs on their verandah,
Reading and hearing music from a tiny transistor.

Their isolation is almost visible :
Blue light on snow or sour milk in a cheese-cloth
Resembles their mysterious element.
They pickle herrings he catches, eat sauerkraut
And make love on cold concrete in the afternoons;
Eaters of yoghurt, they enjoy austere pleasures.

At night oil lamps burn in their small windows
And blocks of pressed peat glow in a simple fireplace.
Arc lamps on the new refinery at the point
Answer their lights; there is blackness and the sound of surf.
They are so alike that they have no need to speak,
Like oppressed orphans who have won a fierce privacy.

Under a Roof

It'll piss all evening now. From next door
The usual man and woman stuff rants on, then fades;
And I know she'll soon be moaning, climbing her little register
Of ecstasy till quiet settles back like dust,
Like rain, among shadows without furniture.

There was a mattress on bare floorboards when I came,
But now I own a bed, a table, and a chair
In a house where no one knows each other's name,
A zone where gardens overgrow and privet rankles—
It stinks in summer and it blinds the panes.

Cats wail at night among the weeds and bricks,
Prowl rusted fire-escapes that lose themselves
In hedges turned to scrub. Exile in the sticks
Is where I've ended up, under wet slates
Where gas flames dry the air and the meter clicks.

The girl I had scared easily. She saw
The dead bareness of the floor, her body near
Both it and mine, so dressed and left the raw,
Rough room I'd brought her to. Up here I'm free
And know a type of power, a certain kind of law.

Noises, the smell of meals, the sounds that bodies make,
All reach me here, drifting from other rooms.
And what I *know* is how much longer it will take
For thoughts and love to change themselves from these
Than rain and rooms to find their senseless lake.

Incognito

A railway halt a long way from Moscow.
Wide *versts* of flat land and some bunched trees
Smeared dark green by rain blurring the window.
Cold air cut in as she opened it and peered through.
'Look !' she said, 'they've lamps on already,
And they're giving tea there to the engine crew.
What a pity we can't join them, think
Of the warm stove and that samovar !'

He looked up at her face that shone white
In the cold air. It was otherwise dark
In the carriage, and he felt he belonged
To that absence of light.

A Traveller

'To me,' he said, 'it was a town
of infinite tedium !
How somehow second-rate it all was !'
We began, then, to understand
a life lived as a search,
suitcases lugged between Americas
and Soviet republics
all found wanting.
What was true of that town
was true of the whole world :
in small cathedral towns, university cities
where old stonework basked distinctly
on clear days,
there was always that same feeling
of it all being so much worn,
movable scenery,
upright shadows in light.

God was not in fire from the air,
nor in tremors rattling the clerestories;
at his elbow, a soft voice
whispered like surf in a shell :
'A word in your ear, friend,
what are you up to? are you well?'
That other voice, not quite his own,
advised :
'Mortal slime, sir, mortal slime.'
Then he would see the tall Swede,
with wide eyes and her smile,
flickering long legs as she stalked
to a smart village—

delicatessens and coffee shops
in mews of clean houses,
blue sky on the panes
of luxury flats.

Ballywaire

My loathsome uncle chews his rasher,
My aunt is mother, pouring tea,
And this is where I live : a town
On the wrong side of the border.

A town the mountain simplifies
To spires and roofs, a bridge that spans
The river—distance shines it—and joins
Packed rural terraces. They're workless,
Costive as the smell of groceries.

Through gunfire, night arrests and searches—
The crossroads loony smashed to bits—
I keep myself intact. My body purifies.
I'll never use it.

The air greys and lights come on
In curtained parlours, our clock ticks
By last year's calendar. The quiet.
An oleograph of Pity in each kitchen.
My heart is stone. I will not budge.

Fin de Siècle

The lake glistens. It is so smooth
Like the green lawns rising to her house,
A house of windows and uncounted rooms.
The hot air trembles, a shimmer of queer-eyed sprats.
The dead are webbing through the afternoon.
That silver pond is all there is between
The man who gazes at the linen girl
(She soothes the heated grass)
And the girl who strolls through this preserve
Of calmness where an absolute forbids
The man to scull across the light
And kiss a girl who seems too cool.

Rare visitors, they are the mists
Of wasted loves, erotic distances
That subtilized their blood and kept them pure.
The beeches in this green demesne,
The dovecote by the summer-house,
Will never tell how when a culture sends
A hopeless man to love a drifting girl,
Then never lets them touch or kiss,
Its selfish flowers have begun to stink.

Free Colour

Evenings after rain; tenants of the rooms
Chew rinsed lettuce and watch the street.
Leading his thin mongrel by a scarf
The thin tramp stares back at a girl
Who is walking, in yellow clogs, towards town.

A grey van slurs to a stop, the bell rings
And Miss Roper watches another antique
Being carried off by the dealer.
Greener than salad, wet new leaves
Sway against the black trunks of the trees;
She wraps her cardigan and hurries in.

The van, sliding in washed light from the kerb,
Overtakes the girl who is marching
Through a green dampness in yellow clogs.

A Desert Development

Theirs is a tight love, these two men
Who live in a metal bungalow
On a sandy patch. Potash and soda,
Blue water and a dry light in the still room
A thousand miles from the sea.
Recent aluminium, everything here is new.

The motel swimming pool is deserted.
A white block stands in the blue sky
Where a vapour trail creates itself
Miles high. Its accurate chalking
A strayed whim that streaks smoothly
Through their extraordinary afternoons.

Newness

Cool to our bodies, the fresh linen pleats
And valances that met our eyes then.

He pressed my hand, my lover, my husband;
Held them both underwater in the wide bowl.

It was still night when I heard
The tramp of clogs to the mill.
Frost on the cobbles, I thought;
Hard wood is worn by the stone,
So is stone by the softness of feet.

In Antrim

Her son is sick and she clears it up.
In twenty years, though he smiles,
He's spoken
Maybe ten different words to her.

The lough's dying, the road's empty.
Near a derelict, twenties bungalow
I watch them from a distance—
Mother, brother.

Young Funerals

A nameless visual.
A series of walls, covered windows,
Doors opening into the shared street.
The terrace brings out its dead.

The girl's small coffin, a new glossiness,
Moving through a windy afternoon.

Two doors down, the boy is dying
In his bedroom. It takes months.

When the thin blinds are drawn
I'll hurry past on the other side.
They must not touch me, these deaths.

His parents are names, a different number.
Their front room is photographs and wept shadows,
An empty shop that gives away misery.

Seaside House

There's a row of holiday paperbacks on the shelf,
Old *Penguins* with orange covers, their pages softening
In the damp and tracing a lost smell.
The smell of an incomplete return,
A departure that doubled back on itself.

Detected through salt windows, this emptiness
Attracts no one who peers into its low room.
Why should it? Those quaint mysteries,
Like the accents the stars once spoke in,
Offer only a parental strangeness.

Arthur

Everyone's got someone who gave them oranges,
Sovereigns or rubbed florins,
Who wore bottle-green blazers, smoked
A churchwarden pipe on St. Swithin's day,
And mulled their ale by dousing red-hot pokers
In quart jars.
But you, you're different.
You pushed off before the millions wrapped their puttees on
And ran away to sea, the prairies, New York
Where they threw you in jail when you told someone
Your blond hair made you a German spy.
After the telegram demanding
Your birth certificate
No one on the Island knew anything about you
Until the Armistice brought a letter
From a wife they'd never heard of.
You'd left her with the baby.
She wanted money.
You were somewhere in South America
In the greatest freedom, the freedom
Of nothing-was-ever-heard-of-him-since.

So I see you sometimes
Paddling up the Orinoco or the River Plate
With rifle, trusty mongrel and native mistress,
Passing cities of abandoned stucco
Draped with lianas and anacondas,
Passing their derelict opera houses
Where Caruso used to warble
Among a million bottles of imported bubbly.
Or else I watch you among the packing-case republics,
Drinking rum at the seafront in Buenos Aires
And waiting for your luck to change;
The warm sticky nights, the news from Europe,

Then the war criminals settling like bats
In the greasy darkness.

Your sister thought she saw your face once
In a crowd scene—
She went to the cinema for a week, watching
For your pale moment. She thinks
You're still alive, sitting back
On the veranda of your hacienda,
My lost great uncle, the blond
Indestructible dare-devil
Who was always playing truant and jumping
Off the harbour wall.

What I want to know is
How you did it.
How you threw off an inherited caution
Or just never knew it.
I think your grave is lost
In the mush of a tropical continent.
You are a memory that blipped out.
And though they named you from the king
Who's supposed to wake and come back
Some day,
I know that if you turned up on my doorstep,
An old sea dog with a worn leather belt
And a face I'd seen somewhere before,
You'd get no welcome.
I'd want you away.

Bradley the Last Idealist

For some reason he never actually taught
Anyone; said a nervous complication
Prevented him, which was why his scout brought
Him over to Savoy each long vacation.
There, every morning on his own, he caught
A cable-car up into the mountains
Where he convalesced on beds of gentians.

Surrounded by blue sky and clouds, he lay
Intently staring into the far distance,
His rapt mind transfixed on Mont Blanc all day
Until absolutely locked in a deep white trance.
He left everything behind him then—the clay,
The cats, books, gowns, nodding domes and misty spires,
Those vulgar details and those Cretan liars.

At nights in term, obscured from gentlemen and God,
He clipped a torch to his air-gun, put his hat
On and prowled stealthily around the dark quad
For cats, his aim utterly accurate—
An absolute guaranteed by torch and tripod.
Then, relishing those brief feline terrors,
He would squeeze gently into their green mirrors.

The College Newsletter

Each year now, relayed from several past addresses,
It finds its way to me and is never expected.
Like an old loyalty it claims more than just money
For cramped extensions to its stone acre.
It asks that I belong and says that somewhere
There is a line of skeletons I'm pleased to know,
A dream of living among books and wine.

Turning the pages I note that Bunter's married.
We got a bump in Torpids, that shit's joined Reuters,
Old Baxen-fyffe-Baines who came up
In 1902 is regrettably dead,
The Turl is closed to traffic now
Whence the quiet of the quad is much enhanced,
Alas we're bottom of the Norrington again.

Was this ever more than just a gloomy building
Where I ate some meals and read the papers?
The kind of dump that sour aesthetes
Stranded up north among a working people
Long to belong to? Where they would really fit?
The golden community, its tides of light
Fresh on carved stone's superb distinctions?

I wouldn't know. I thought this was a tie
I'd broken long ago—as if I'd pay them money !
I met a couple of the dons, I think—
Dim men in gowns who stuffed themselves with food
Most nights. But why some ancient fellow
Should think I care about his bits of stone?
The mind is better than the thing itself.

Responsibilities

No way now, there's no way.
Geometry and rose-beds,
The light changing on the hill
Where two gravediggers glance up.
Her tears fell into your silence.

The air starved when the earth pushed.
Something made a fuck of things;
Straight and bare is all it is.
No. I kept you off, my brother,
And I'll never see your face.

Firelight

Framed among ornaments, one by one
you've started to become
the faces of dead people—those
who died young, who made nothing
happen outside us, and the old
seated in armchairs like thrones,
prepared to die, but smiling.

It closes in, like the evenings
silting the tall windows.
Your voices brimmed here, but now,
dead ones, I visit you with those
glances we know. Ask me how
we got to this firelight and I'll sing
in your voices, softly, of absences.

Monumental Mason

Working beside a cemetery,
Chiselling dates and names
On cheap slabs of marble
In the lighted shop window,
His meek power makes us nervous.

With his back to the street,
He cuts them in, these loves
The dead can't care about.
In his washed-out overalls
He is less a person

Than a function. People
Have grown used to him
As he sits intently
Gilding the incised letters,
A mason, displayed.

*Doris, Beloved Wife
And Mother,* or *Agnes
RIP*, their names are
Public, but we forget them,
Glimpsing a tenderness

On bald stone, some dead letters;
Or, when the traffic lulls,
Hearing from next door
The undertaker's tap, tap,
Answer his vigilant chinking.

Also an Evasion

Also an evasion, the journal entries, the weather notes
That may be useful somewhen.

Not tasks, not work, they're just a pottering
About the time I own.
A way of forgetting what the leaves mean,
The cries of children in gardens
Softing like white songs
That'll never reach these glazed boards.